Ladybug, Ladybug

for my sister, Sylvia

Unicorn is a registered trademark of
Dutton Children's Books.

Library of Congress number 88-14852
ISBN 0-14-054543-3

First published in the United States by
Dutton Children's Books,
a division of Penguin Books USA Inc.
375 Hudson Street, New York, New York 10014

Originally published in Great Britain by
Andersen Press Ltd.
Printed in Hong Kong
First Unicorn Edition 1992
10 9 8 7 6 5 4 3

Ladybug, Ladybug

RUTH BROWN

A Puffin Unicorn

DUTTON CHILDREN'S BOOKS
NEW YORK

Ladybug, ladybug, fly away home.
Your house is on fire, your children are gone.

House all afire? Can it be so?
Poor ladybug doesn't know which way to go.

Ladybug, ladybug, blown by the breeze,
Over the wheat field, into the trees.

Ladybug, ladybug, lands in some smoke.
There's really a fire, it isn't a joke.

Ladybug, ladybug, fly away, fly.
That frog has a hungry look in his eye.

Ladybug, ladybug, which way to go?
Old snail is friendly, but he doesn't know.

Ladybug, ladybug, better not pause
So close to those dangerous, razor-sharp claws.

Ladybug, ladybug, pass the pig by.
He's too full to help and too lazy to try.

Ladybug, ladybug, go to the crow.
Ask him the way, he'll probably know.

Ladybug, ladybug, deep in the wood.
Squirrel can't help, but she wishes she could.

Ladybug, ladybug, once again blown.
Is it too late? Are your children all gone?

Ladybug, ladybug, off in a rush.
Follow the bees to your blackberry bush.

Ladybug, ladybug, all's clear at last.
Fly to your children, fly home to them fast.

Ladybug, ladybug, safely at home.
It isn't on fire and your children aren't gone.

They're all sound asleep, snug in their nest.
Ladybug joins them. At last she can rest.